It was a river.

On the bank oppo
r's edge,
was a dark hole. At t was
twinkling. Bright eyes ....ed face.
The Water Rat.

"Hullo, Mole!" said the Water Rat.

"Hullo, Rat," said Mole, shyly.

"Would you like to come on the water?" said Rat,
untying a little blue boat. Mole's heart went out to
that boat.

"I've never been in a boat before."

Rat was open-mouthed. "What *have* you been doing, then? There's nothing – absolutely nothing – better than simply messing about in boats."

They drifted down the river together.

Mole waggled his toes from sheer happiness.

"What's that?" asked Mole, pointing at some thick, dark trees.

"The Wild Wood," said Rat. "We don't go there much."

"Aren't the people *nice* there?" asked Mole.

"Well ..." said Rat. "Badger's all right. But the weasels and stoats – you just can't trust them."

"And beyond the Wild Wood, where it's blue and dim?"

"That's the Wide World," said Rat. "And it doesn't matter at all."

They moored in a backwater with brown, snaky tree roots.

Rat lifted out a fat wicker picnic basket and laid a tablecloth.

"Cold chicken," Rat said. "Coldhamcoldbeef pickledgherkinscresssandwichesgingerbeerand ..."

"Oh, stop!" cried Mole.

They ate.

And ate.

And got fuller.

And dreamier.

And more peaceful.

Until –

A rower splashed past in a brand-new boat.

Rat sighed.

"Who's that?" asked Mole.

"Toad," said Rat. The plump figure was trying his hardest, but kept rolling and tipping.

"He's a good fellow, but given to crazes. First it was sailing. Then house-boating, and now ..." Rat shook his head as Toad disappeared in a spray of water.

The afternoon sun was getting low.

"Home," Rat said.

"Ratty," Mole said, as they climbed into the boat, "I want to row!"

"It's not as easy as it looks, my friend."

For a while, Rat rowed and hummed and made up poetry.

And Mole watched. Mole was full of lunch – and pride. Suddenly, he jumped up and snatched the oars, which sent Rat flying.

"Stop it, you idiot! You'll have us over!"

Mole dug at the water with an oar – and missed. His legs flew up and then ... Splosh!

The water was cold.

And *very* wet.

It sang in Mole's ears as he sank.

Down.

Down …

A firm paw gripped the back of Mole's neck.

Rat lifted the squashy lump of misery onto the bank.

"I'm very sorry for my ungrateful behaviour," said Mole, in a broken voice.

"What's a little wet to a Water Rat?" said Rat cheerily. "Now, if you really want to learn the ways of the river, you must come and stay at mine."

So that was the first night that Mole fell asleep to the lapping of the river and the whispering of the wind among the willows.

2 THE OPEN ROAD

Spring turned into summer, and Mole was still staying.

"Ratty," he said one bright June day, "could we visit your friend, Mr Toad?"

"Certainly," said the good-natured Rat. "Such a lovable animal. He's not clever, but we can't all be geniuses."

Toad Hall was a handsome red-brick house with wide lawns down to the water's edge. There were many splendid boats in Toad's boat-house – all unused.

"Ah," said Rat, as they arrived. "He's tired of boating, then."

"Hooray!" Toad cried, spotting them and not waiting for introductions. "I've finally discovered the Real Thing. Follow me!" He led them to the stable yard. "Look!" It was a painted caravan. All shiny-new and sunshine-yellow.

"The open road," Toad said, "the dusty highway. Travel, change, excitement. We leave this afternoon."

"*We?*" said Rat.

"You can't just stick to your river and live your life in a hole," said Toad. "I'm going to show you the world. Make an animal of you, my boy!"

"I *am* going to stick to my river," said Rat. "And what's more, Mole's going to stick with me."

"I am," said Mole loyally, though the caravan looked thrilling.

When Rat saw Mole's shining eyes, he changed his mind. He hated disappointing people.

So Toad caught the old grey horse (who preferred the paddock and needed a great deal of catching) and they set off.

It was a golden afternoon. Birds whistled and rabbits said, "Oh my," as they passed. When they finally stopped for the night, Toad talked about his plans for the future, and the stars got fuller and larger all around them.

"This is the life!" said Toad, when they tumbled into their bunks at last. "Talk about your old river!"

"I *don't* talk about it," said Rat, and then added in a lower tone, "but I *think* about it all the time."

"Shall we run away?" Mole whispered. "Go home together?"

"Thanks awfully," said Rat. "But we have to stick by Toad. He's not safe by himself."

As they travelled the following day, they heard a warning hum behind them. It was like the drone of a distant bee, coming at them with incredible speed.

Poop, poop!

A magnificent, breath-snatching motorcar roared past, flinging clouds of dust.

The horse reared and plunged. There was a heart-rending crash and the caravan landed in a ditch.

Rat shook his fist at the departing car. "I'll have the law on you!"

Toad, meanwhile, sat in a trance on
the dusty road. "Poop, poop ..."

"Are you coming to help us?" yelled Rat from
the ditch.

"Glorious sight," said the spellbound Toad.

"Stop being an idiot!" cried Mole.

"Horrid little caravan," said Toad. "Common
yellow caravan."

"Now look here, Toad," said Rat, sharply,
"we're going to complain about that car."

"Complain?" said Toad. "About that heavenly vision?"

With the caravan broken beyond repair, they'd no
choice but to walk home.

The next day, Toad ordered a large and very
expensive motorcar.

3 THE WILD WOOD

Summer became autumn. Mole wanted to meet
Mr Badger.

Rat put him off. "Badger will turn up, but you
must only take him *as* you find him and *when* you
find him."

"Couldn't we call on him?"

"Out of the question. He lives in the Wild Wood."

Mole waited.

And waited.

Mr Badger did not turn up. So one steel-grey afternoon, Mole set out for the Wild Wood all by himself. Nature was deep in her winter slumber. The countryside lay bare and leafless around him. Mole liked the hardness of it. It was strong and simple.

There was nothing in the wood to alarm him at first. Then, as dusk came, the light drained away like floodwater and the faces appeared.

A little evil, wedge-shaped face, looking at Mole from a hole. When he turned to confront it, it vanished.

He quickened his pace.

Another hole. Another face. Then hundreds of them.
He swung off the path.

Which is when the whistling began.

And the pattering …

A rabbit rushed at him: "Get out of here, you fool!"

The pattering increased. The whole wood seemed to
be hunting him – chasing, closing in.

In panic, Mole began to run – blindly. He finally
collapsed, panting and trembling, in the hollow of
an old beech tree.

Rat, meanwhile, woke from his doze by the fire. "Moly?" he called.

Moly wasn't there.

Moly's cap was missing. And his Wellington boots.

Outside, Rat saw mud tracks leading towards the Wild Wood. Without hesitation, Rat marched straight into that wood. The wicked faces disappeared immediately at the sight of the fearless Rat.

"Moly," Rat called out cheerfully. "Moly – where are you?"

It was an hour before a feeble voice replied:
"Ratty – is that really you?"

Rat followed the sound and found the exhausted
Mole in a hollow.

"Oh Rat, I've been so frightened."

"I quite understand," said Rat, soothingly.
"But you shouldn't really have come here by yourself.
Home now … Uh oh," he added, sticking his nose out
of the hollow.

"What's up?"

"Snow's up," replied Rat. "Or rather down.
It's snowing hard."

Mole looked out. All the holes and hollows were
vanishing under a gleaming carpet of white. It looked
too delicate to be trodden on by rough feet.

They set out bravely, but the snow buried all
landmarks. There seemed to be no beginning – and no
end – to the wood. Mole tripped, squealing as he fell.

"Oh my leg!"

"Poor old Mole," said Rat kindly, reaching for his handkerchief. "Oh that's a clean cut. That was never made by a tree stump."

"Well, never mind what done it," said Mole, forgetting his grammar in his pain. "It hurts whatever done it!"

But Rat was suddenly busy shovelling snow. "Hooray!" he cried. "Look!"

It was a door scraper.

"Who dances a jig round a door scraper?"
asked Mole.

"Don't you see, you dim animal?" said Rat.

"I see that a very careless person has left his door
scraper in the middle of the wood where it's sure to trip
everyone up," replied Mole.

"Come on," said Rat. "DIG."

After ten minutes hard work, a solid little
door appeared beneath the snow. The name on
the doorplate was: Mr Badger.

4 MR BADGER

Mole pulled the doorbell and they heard shuffling footsteps.

The door opened a crack, revealing a long snout and a pair of sleepy, blinking eyes. "Now the very next time this happens," said a gruff voice, "I shall be exceedingly angry."

"It's me," cried Rat, "and my friend Mole. We've lost our way in the snow."

"Ratty – my dear little man," exclaimed Badger, in quite a different tone.

"Come along in, both of you, at once."

Badger wore a long dressing gown, worn-out slippers, and carried a candle.

"It's not the sort of night for small animals to be out," he said, in a fatherly way.

He led them down a shabby passage, into the warmth of a large, fire-lit kitchen. Rows of spotless plates winked from the dresser. Meats and baskets of eggs hung from the rafters. It seemed a place where heroes might feast.

The kindly Badger removed their wet clothes, fetched rugs and bathed Mole's wound. Warm and dry at last, the animals began to think the Wild Wood was just some half-forgotten dream.

23

They didn't know how hungry they were, until they sat down to supper. Conversation was impossible with their mouths so full. But eventually, when Badger saw they were fit to burst, he said: "How's old Toad?"

"Gone from bad to worse," said Rat. "Had another car crash last week. His seventh!"

"And he's been in hospital three times," Mole put in.

"We're his friends, Badger," said Rat. "Shouldn't we do something?"

5 MR TOAD

As soon as the snows passed, the friends went to
Toad Hall. On the driveway was a huge, red,
brand-new motorcar.

Toad swaggered down the steps. He wore goggles,
cap, gloves and an enormous overcoat.

"Hello!" he cried. "You're just in time for a – er – jolly … "

"Take off those ridiculous clothes," said Badger.

"Shan't!" said Toad, with great spirit.

So they marched him inside – with Toad kicking
and yelling – and removed the motor-clothes
themselves. When he was finally more *Toad* and less
Terror of the Highway, Badger led him into the library
and closed the door.

"That's no good!" Rat said. "*Talking* won't cure him!"

An hour later, Badger brought out a limp Toad. His legs were wobbling. There were tears on his cheeks.

"He's seen the error of his ways," Badger declared. "He's sorry."

There was a pause.

"Sorry?" Toad looked this way and that. "I'm not sorry. It was all … simply GLORIOUS!"

"You backsliding animal!" cried Badger.

"And the moment I see another poop-poop, off I'll go again!"

The friends had no choice but to take Toad upstairs and lock him in his bedroom.

"It's for your own good, Toady," said Rat.

Toady didn't think so. He moaned and built motorcars out of chairs in his room. Then he crashed the chairs and lay – yelling – among the ruins.

After a few weeks, the noise died down.

Toad had taken to his bed.

27

"I'm dying," he said feebly, when Rat came to check on him.

"Dying!" Rat set off at once to get a doctor.

As soon as he'd left, Toad got up, knotted some sheets together and (because the door was still locked) climbed out of the window.

The carefree Toad wandered down to the Red Lion Inn.
A beautiful open-topped car was parked outside.

"I wonder," he said, "if this sort of car starts easily?"

As if in a dream, he found himself in the driver's seat.
A moment later, without any sense of right or wrong,
he was swinging out of the yard. The car ate up street
and road and open country.

Faster and faster.

Toad – the Terror of the Highway!

"A Very Clear Case," said the judge, when the matter finally came to court. He peered at the trembling Toad. "Stealing a car, dangerous driving *and* resisting arrest. What's the worst penalty we can give this thug?"

"20 years, m'lud."

At once, the guards fell upon Toad, dragging him (shrieking, kicking, protesting) to the remotest dungeon of the grimmest castle in the land.

The door clanged shut behind him.

6 TOAD'S ADVENTURES

"This is the end of everything!" said Toad, flinging himself to the prison floor. "At least, it's the end of Toad, which is the same thing. Oh clever Rat, sensible Mole, wise Badger and – " he broke off, sobbing – "forgotten Toad!"

The shouting and the bitter tears went on for a good few weeks before the jailer's daughter took pity on Toad and brought him a steaming plate of cabbage. The divine smell made Toad dry his eyes.

"I've an aunt who's a washerwoman," said the girl.

"Oh, how fascinating," said Toad, tucking in.

31

"No, listen … " The girl whispered something
in his ear.

"Escape from the castle dressed as
a washerwoman?" exploded Toad. "Because I'm
the same shape *as a washerwoman*?!"

"You proud, ungrateful animal," said the girl. "I was
only trying to help."

And Toad saw that she was right. So, when
the washerwoman came to call, he gave her some
coins in exchange for her clothes. Then he bound
and gagged her (so she wouldn't get into trouble later)
and walked out of the prison wearing a cotton dress,
an apron and a bonnet tied under his chin.

The outside air made him feel dizzy.

Or was it the snorting of trains?

A station!

Toad's spirits rose as he went to buy a ticket. Home.
Home! He put his hand into his waistcoat pocket.
But he wasn't wearing his waistcoat anymore. He was
wearing a dress.

Oh, miserable Toad. No keys, watch, matches,
pencil-case Or MONEY.

He wandered down the platform, full of despair. Soon they would discover his escape and the hunt would begin.

The steam engine was being wiped by a large man with an oilcan.

"Hullo?" said the engine driver. "What's the trouble?"

"Oh, sir," said Toad, crying heartily, "I'm a poor, unhappy washerwoman who's lost her money and can't get home."

"And have you got children waiting?" asked the engine driver.

"Hundreds of them," sobbed Toad, "all hungry and playing with matches, no doubt … "

"Well, hop up then."

The train roared away. The countryside flew past. Just as Toad was thinking, FREE AT LAST, another train appeared on the rails behind them.

"They're gaining on us fast!" cried the engine driver. "And what strange people!"

Policemen swinging truncheons.

Guards swinging handcuffs.

"Stop! STOP!" they shouted.

Toad fell to his knees among the coals and confessed everything.

The engine driver looked very stern. "I fear you've been a wicked Toad. But I don't like being bossed about by people. Especially when I'm on my engine. So cheer up, Toad. We may beat them yet!"

The engine driver piled on the coals and drove like a madman. Once he'd lost the other train as they passed through a tunnel, he shut off steam and pulled on the brakes.

"Jump!" he yelled.

7 THE FURTHER ADVENTURES OF TOAD

Toad jumped.

S
    l
        i
                d.

Fell.

Down the embankment.

THUMP onto a canal towpath.

As he dusted himself off, he spotted a horse pulling a barge.

"Nice day, ma'am," called the beefy barge-woman.

Toad said politely that it might be if it wasn't for the bruises and being a long way from his home and his children and his washing business.

"Oh, you do washing, do you!" exclaimed
the barge-woman.

"Oh – I love it," said Toad. "I'm never so happy
as when I have both arms in the washtub!"

"Well, jump aboard," said the barge-woman.
Toad was just thinking, *Toad's luck again*, when
the woman added: "I'll swap you a lift home for a bit
of washing. I love washing, but I don't have the time."

She directed him to a heap of dirty clothes in
the cabin.

Toad shuddered.

"There's a tub and soap there – and a kettle on the stove."

"Here, why don't you wash," said Toad, "and I'll steer?"

"No, no. Wouldn't want to stop you doing the washing you're so fond of."

Toad was cornered.

He fetched the tub, the soap and a few garments. Then, for a good half-hour, he got crosser and crosser. He tried slapping, he tried punching, but the clothes remained stubbornly grey. Worse still, his beautiful paws began to get all crinkly.

The barge-woman laughed. "Never washed so much as a dishcloth in your life, have you?"

Toad's temper finally boiled over. "You common, low, *ugly* barge-woman!" he shouted. "I'm a very well-known Toad and I will NOT be laughed at!"

"Why," said the barge-woman, looking under his bonnet, "so you are. A nasty, crawly toad. In my nice, clean barge too!"

She shot out a mighty arm and grasped Toad by the leg. Then Toad's world turned upside-down. He was flying.

"Put yourself in the mangle," the barge-woman yelled, "and iron your face! Then you might make a decent-looking toad."

Toad landed hard on the bank, bounced across the towpath and plopped into the next-door river.

Just outside Rat's house.

8 TOAD'S RETURN

Rat put out a neat, brown paw, gripped Toad
by the neck and heaved him inside.

"Oh, Ratty," cried Toad, "I've been through such
terrible times since I saw you and … "

"And," Rat interrupted, "you can go upstairs,
take off that ridiculous frock and try to come back
down dressed like a gentleman."

Toad wanted to argue but then caught sight of himself in the hat-stand mirror. He went upstairs very humbly.

He returned to a beautiful lunch.

"Afterwards," he told Rat, "I'll be strolling down to Toad Hall."

"So you haven't heard?" cried Rat.

"Heard what?" said Toad, turning pale.

"How – when you were *away* – the Wild Wooders took over your house?"

Two great tears welled up and spilt from Toad's eyes.

"The River-bankers stuck up for you, of course, but the Wild Wooders said it served you right. The weasels and ferrets and stoats swarmed in and took over the place. As I speak, they're eating your food and drinking your … "

"Right!" exclaimed Toad, grabbing a stick. "I'll jolly well see about that!"

"It's no good … " called Rat.

But Toad had already left.

He marched down the road muttering, the stick over his shoulder. Standing guard at the gate of Toad Hall was a long, mean ferret.

With a gun.

"Who goes there?" said the ferret, sharply.

"Stuff and nonsense!" said Toad, angrily.

Without a word, the ferret brought the gun up to his shoulder. Toad (sensibly) dropped down flat in the road.

BANG!

The bullet whistled over Toad's head.

Toad scrambled back to Rat's house – a slightly wiser beast.

Rat was just telling Toad how hard Badger and Mole had worked to try to defend Toad Hall, when the pair arrived.

"Hooray, Toady!" cried Mole. "How clever of you to escape jail!"

"Clever?" said Toad. "Not really. I only broke out of the strongest prison in England and captured a train and a barge and humbugged people … "

"Toad!" Badger said sternly. "You're a bad, troublesome animal. Aren't you ashamed of yourself?" He paused. "Still, it doesn't mean the stoats and the weasels can steal your house."

The creatures all started shouting over each other about how to win back Toad Hall.

"Stop," said Badger, at last. "I've a secret to share."

The creatures waited.

"There – is – an – underground – passage, from the riverbank, right up into Toad Hall."

"Nonsense, Badger," said Toad. "If there was a passage, I'd know about it!"

Badger glared at him. "Your father didn't tell you – because you can't keep a secret!"

47

"Well," said Toad, trying not to sulk, "how does it help us?"

"Tonight," said Badger, "it's the Chief Weasel's birthday. There'll be guards posted, of course. But most of the animals will be in the dining hall – which is where the passage emerges."

"We'll creep out quietly … " said Mole.

"And DO 'EM OVER!" shouted Toad.

"So that's settled," said Badger. "Now I'm just going to take 40 winks." And he put a handkerchief over his face.

9 THE BATTLE FOR TOAD HALL

The friends gathered pistols and sticks and sticking-plaster (just in case) and set out through the low, damp passageway. Toad shivered with fear – until he heard the noise of the party above. Then he became MAD.

Badger put his shoulder to the trap door.

"All together now!" he cried, and flung the door wide.

My!

What a squealing and squeaking and screeching there was.

Glass and china crashed to the floor as those four Heroes strode into the room. The mighty Badger, whiskers bristling, club held high. Mole, black and grim, shaking his stick and shouting his awful war cry: "A Mole! A Mole!" Rat, desperate and determined, his belt bulging with weapons. And Toad, swollen to twice his normal size, leaping and whooping. There were only four of them but, to the panic-stricken Wild Wooders, the hall seemed full of monstrous animals, black, brown and yellow, all shrieking and bawling.

Terrified weasels sprang madly at windows …

Ferrets rushed for the fireplace and got jammed up the chimney …

Toad made straight for the Chief Weasel.

It was all over in a moment. The enemy howling as they fled into the night.

The room was clear.

"Well, that did 'em," said Toad.

The friends congratulated each other and sat down to dinner.

"Tomorrow," said Badger, "you must hold a feast to celebrate, Toad. It's quite expected."

Toad's chest puffed up as he imagined the fine speeches he'd make, the songs he'd sing.

Toad – *Great Weasel Defeater*!

"But no speeches," said Rat.

"What?" cried Toad. "Not even a little song?"

"No," said Rat firmly. "Your speeches and songs are all boasting and … "

"Gas," finished Badger.

"This is a hard, hard world," said Toad.

The following day, an hour before the banquet, Toad went to his room. He locked the door, drew the curtains and arranged the chairs in a semi-circle. In an uplifting voice to his imaginary audience, he sang:

There was smashing in of window and crashing in of door,
There was chasing off of weasels that fainted on the floor,
When Toad – came – home!
The trumpeters are tooting and the soldiers are saluting
And the cannon they are shooting and the motorcars
are hooting,
As the Hero – comes.

Followed by a great many other verses.

Then he heaved a deep sigh, brushed his hair and came downstairs to his guests. And, when they begged him for a speech, longed for just a little song, he shook his head gently.

He was, his friends agreed, a changed Toad.

A Map

The
Wild Wood

The
River Bank

54

Toad Hall

Ideas for reading

Written by Clare Dowdall, PhD
Lecturer and Primary Literacy Consultant

Reading objectives:
- draw inferences such as inferring characters' feelings, thoughts and motives from their actions, and justifying inferences with evidence
- predict what might happen from details stated and implied
- discuss and evaluate how authors use language, including figurative language, considering the impact on the reader

Spoken language objectives:
- Use spoken language to develop understanding through speculating, hypothesising, imagining and exploring ideas

Curriculum Links: Science – Living things and their habitats; PSHE – friendship

Resources: art materials for painting/ drawing; pencils and paper; ICT for research

Build a context for reading
- Ask children whether they've heard of the classic story *The Wind in the Willows*, and to share anything they know about it. Explain what a willow tree is and where it usually grows (by a river).
- Look at the front cover together. Ask children to identify the creatures and describe what they can see. Discuss what sort of story this might be, where it might be set and what might happen.
- Read the blurb aloud. Ask children to suggest what kind of creature a "Wild Wooder" might be.

Understand and apply reading strategies
- Ask children to read Chapter 1 to find out about Mole and Rat, and how their story begins. When they've finished, ask them to recount what has happened and to predict what might happen next. Establish that Mole and Rat have become friends who'll have adventures together.